Mrs. McNosh and the Great Big Squash

by Sarah Weeks

pictures by Nadine Bernard Westcott

A Laura Geringer Book
HarperFestival®
A Division of HarperCollins*Publishers*

SQUASH

The first day of spring,
Mrs. Nelly McNosh
went out to her garden
and planted a squash.

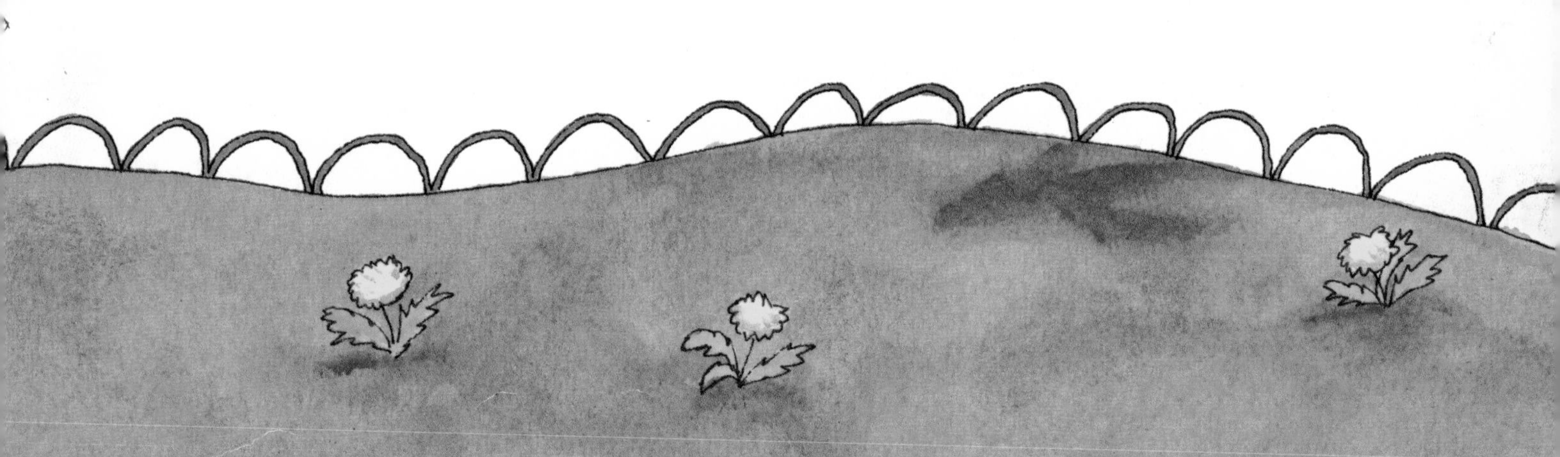

She pushed the seed in
with the tip of her toe,
and the minute she did it,
it started to grow.

SQUASH

At first it was round
and as big as a head—
in fact it looked just like
the paperboy, Fred.

SQUASH

Then it turned yellow
and bumpy and fat.
It rolled from the garden
and flattened the cat.

It knocked over trash cans
and ran over toes.
It twisted the sprinkler
and plugged up the hose.

It crashed through the clothesline
and smashed through the fence,
scaring the pants off two elderly gents.

Poor Nelly was worried.
She said, "Oh my gosh,
there's got to be some way
to slow down this squash."

She slapped it and scolded it,
pinched it and kicked it,
and then she took hold of its stem . . .
and she *picked* it.

"Now what do I do?"
wondered Mrs. McNosh.
"I've got to find something to *do* with this squash.
There isn't a place in the world it will fit.
It's big as a house— Wait," said Nelly,
"that's it!"

And so, by the light
of a big yellow moon,
she scooped and she scraped
with a long-handled spoon.
And when the sun rose,
where was Mrs. McNosh?

Curled up sound asleep

z Z Z Z
z Z Z

in her big yellow squash.